o pants required"
e rear half of the
round the ankles,
and hips) serves
e poodle's joints
e many stylish
pular in France.

Dalmatian

Though its actual origins are not clear, we do
know that the dalmatian is one of the most
recognizable breeds with its distinctive coat.
It has had several different occupations
throughout its history, including border guard dog
and firehouse dog. Puppies are born without spots,
so good looks, as well as wisdom, come with age.

Borzoi

The borzoi's long graceful body and elegant
features may give the impression of an
aristocrat but make no mistake—this hound dog
likes to hunt! They're quick to give chase when
something catches their eye, so be sure to wear
your running shoes when walking a borzoi!

geback

o the list of names
nd) applied to the
nd muscular, the
line of hair running
ters discovered its
other nicknames.

Peruvian Hairless

Its official name (Peruvian Inca Orchid) sounds
like a delicate flower. And while not a flower,
this dog is certainly exotic and requires
special care. Its hairless body needs protection
from the elements (a good sunscreen or sweater).
The upside to no hair? No doggie odor or fleas!

Chihuahua

Since the Chihuahua usually doesn't exceed
six pounds, it's easy to see why some people stash
their pooches in their handbags. But we don't
recommend it! An active dog, it prefers to do
its own walking. While it may be the smallest
breed in the world, the Chihuahua walks tall and is
known for its confident, self-reliant temperament.

First Dog

J. Patrick Lewis and Beth Zappitello

★

Illustrated by Tim Bowers

Sleeping Bear Press™

PUBLISHER

Once upon a time there was a dog tha

was looking for the perfect place to live.

Then one day...

Hmmm, thought Dog. This gives me an idea.

I'll trot across the continents, that's what I'll do.
And if I'm lucky, maybe I'll find the perfect place to live.

So he set off to travel the world.

Dog first arrived in Newfoundland. There he found a...Newfoundland!

She takes to water just like me, Dog barked. Who could ask for more?
Just then Dog remembered. Whoa, I've heard this furry giant
can even be a lifeguard. All I can rescue is my dog toy.

So Dog sailed across the Atlantic Ocean to London, England.
Waddling near Big Ben was a slobbering English bulldog.

He's rough and tough, thought Dog. Did he break that nose in a fight?
I bet he has a sturdy brick home that would be perfect for me
but how could I get any sleep with all that snoring!

So Dog traveled to France. There he saw a standard poodle.

Puffy and poofy and spiffy, Dog marveled. *But who wants to spend all day at the hairdresser's?* Dog decided he just couldn't bring himself to parade around town without pants. So it was off to somewhere new.

In Croatia he thought at first he was seeing spots...

but it was just Dot-to-Dot, a dalmatian, hanging out at the one place dalmatians like best. Dog tried to play tic-tac-paw with her, but how can you have fun with someone whose best friend is a fire truck?

What was waiting for him in Russia? The famous borzoi.

Wow, what an elegant creature. Dog was in awe.
No, the life of the great hunting Russian wolfhound is
not for me. The only thing I love to hunt is my dinner bowl!

In China Dog went in search of the strange-looking shar-pei.

So soft, Dog sighed, but so wrinkly. Not even an iron could get out those wrinkles. And look at that blue-black tongue. It's meant to scare off the evil spirits but I'm afraid of my own shadow!

Next Dog decided to go to Australia, the land down-under, to see a dingo.

After chasing him across the hot desert, Dog thought, *That lone ranger might be wild but he's no party animal. Definitely not the place for me. I need fun, friends, excitement. And whew, this outback sun could roast a doggie burger like shrimp on the barbie. G'day, mate!*

Let's see, Dog wondered, *where else could I find the perfect place to live?*

Dog went to South Africa and met a Rhodesian Ridgeback.

He soon found out that this fido's favorite thing to do is...hunt lions!
What? I like cats, but Rule № 1 is: They have to be smaller than me!
First a cowlick down its back and now a house next to a lion's den?
Dog shuddered. *No thank you.*

Next Dog went back across the Atlantic for a stop in South America.

As soon as he met the Peruvian Hairless, he thought, *Yikes, bald, baby, bald! Put some clothes on, why don't you? Dog brushed up against the creature. Why, her skin feels like it's heated. I can see why she's a pampered pooch— she's a bed-warmer for humans. But I need a room of my own.*

Then Dog traveled north to Mexico—*olé! Si, si,* the Chihuahua.

Muy adorable! cried Dog. She loves to sunbathe, too. But I'd get squished inside a purse. Oh no, I definitely need a house bigger than a lunch box!

At last Dog was worn out from his worldwide travels, and a little sad, too, because he hadn't found the perfect place to live.

He returned to his old neighborhood, walked over to his
favorite park bench, rolled in the grass, and took a nap.

When Dog awoke, he saw that somebody
had left another newspaper on the bench.

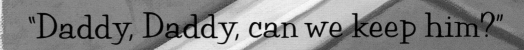

"Daddy, Daddy, can we keep him?"

"YES, WE CAN!"

It is estimated today that there are over four million abandoned dogs in the United States. Abandoned, mistreated or lost, these animals are in desperate need of a loving home. Their lives depend on it. If you and your family can rescue a dog (or a cat), you'll be rewarded with a loving companion for years to come. Or your family or school may consider supporting a local shelter with donations of pet food, toys, and bedding. Check in with your neighborhood shelter to see what they need.

★ ★ ★

To all those in the rescue community whose
tireless efforts save so many wonderful dogs.
J.P.L.

To my own litter, Ajax and Hopper, and my husband, Zap.
With love, Beth

To my friend, Wes
T.B.

Sleeping Bear Press™ • © 2009 Sleeping Bear Press is an imprint of Gale, a part of Cengage Learning. • 310 North Main Street, Suite 300, Chelsea, MI 48118 • www.sleepingbearpress.com • Text Copyright © 2009 J. Patrick Lewis and Beth Zappitello • Illustration Copyright © 2009 Tim Bowers • All rights reserved. No part of this book may be reproduced in any manner without the express written consent of the publisher, except in the case of brief excerpts in critical reviews and articles. • Printed and bound in the United States. • 10 9 8 7 6 5 4 3 2 1 • Library of Congress Cataloging-in-Publication Data • Lewis, J. Patrick. • First dog • J. Patrick Lewis and Beth Zappitello ; [illustrations by] Tim Bowers. -- 1st ed • p. cm. • Summary: Dog travels the world looking for the perfect place to live, meeting dogs of many breeds before finally returning to Washington, D.C., where he learns of a special family seeking a pet to live in their big, white house. • ISBN 978-1-58536-467-1 • [1. Dogs--Fiction. 2. Home--Fiction. 3. Travel--Fiction. 4. White House (Washington, D.C.)--Fiction] I. Zappitello, Beth. II. Bowers, Tim, ill. III. Title. • PZ7.L5866Fir 2009 • [E]--dc22 • 2009002375

Newfoundland

The Newfoundland (Newfie to its closest friends!) loves the water and is an excellent swimmer. But a bathing suit and water wings are not required since this dog has a water-resistant coat and webbed feet. Patient and brave, it's a good thing the Newfoundland is large and likes people—past occupations have included water rescue.

English Bulldog

The bulldog's prizefighter appearance is deceptive; it has a very gentle temperament and is a good family pet. Earplugs can help with the loud snoring and be sure to stock up on towels for the drool. But despite his cuddly nature, don't put him on your lap—bulldogs can weigh 40-50 pounds!

Though it may loo
haircut (Poodle cl
body shaved, bra
and pom-poms lef
a purpose. It help
and organs in co
things, the poodl

Chinese Shar-Pei

While its skin tone may remind you of your old granny, the shar-pei actually loses its wrinkles as it ages (puppies have more wrinkles than adults). But the shar-pei is an old breed and its likeness is said to be found on ancient Chinese pottery.

Dingo

If you want to make friends with a dingo, you'd better do it while he's still a young pup! After the age of 10 weeks, a dingo is better left in the wild. The dingo rarely is aggressive, shies away from humans, and would rather run than fight.

Rhodesi

"Tough guy" can als
(Lion Dog and Afric
Rhodesian Ridgeb
Ridgeback gets its na
down its back. South
skill in hunting lio